The Dragon of Redonda

Frané Lessac
and
Jan Jackson

MACMILLAN
CARIBBEAN

First published 1986 by
MACMILLAN EDUCATION LTD
London and Basingstoke
*Associated companies and representatives in Accra, Banjul,
Cairo, Dar es Salaam, Delhi, Freetown, Gaborone, Harare,
Hong Kong, Johannesburg, Kampala, Lagos, Lahore, Lusaka,
Mexico City, Nairobi, São Paulo, Tokyo*

ISBN 0–333–41683–X

16   15   14   13   12   11   10   9   8   7
05   04   03   02   01   00   99   98   97   96

Printed in Hong Kong

A catalogue record for this book is available from the
British Library.

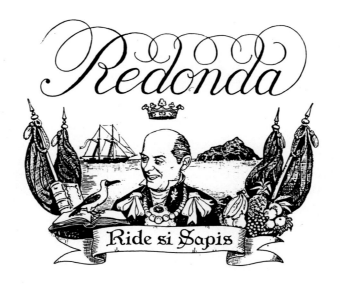

Ride si Sapis

Foreword

Redonda, in case you do not know, is a real island. It is a mile long, a thousand feet high, and is surrounded by the beautiful blue Caribbean Sea.

If that was not enough, there has been a King of Redonda since 1865. The present King has been asked to write these few words. He is happy to do so because although he thought he knew his kingdom well – even the deep dark cave that is in a high and secret part of the island – he has not met Rupert, who comes into this splendid story, and he would like to introduce him. (One of the boring things about being a King is that one seldom meets really interesting dragons like Rupert.)

The pictures are splendid too, but perhaps they make Redonda rather prettier than it really is, for in fact it can be a quite frightening place, especially at night under the full moon when the wind (or could it be Rupert?) roars betweeen the peaks, and the waves thunder and foam over the dark round rocks at the foot of the steep cliffs.

Humans once lived on Redonda, but now it is the home of thousands of sea birds, wild goats with long trailing beards, and the seldom-seen Burrowing Owl. And that is how the present King wishes it to remain, for there are too few places where birds and animals are left in peace by man.

The children in the story were welcome there, of course, otherwise they would never have met Rupert. Now it is *your* chance to do so, in the pages of this book, so I shall leave you to get on with it.

Enjoy this story of my island!

Juan II

Once upon a time, a young boy named Bo was out fishing in his little wooden boat with his friends Jane and Layla when they were suddenly caught in a wild storm. The rain fell and the winds blew. Angry waves with peaked white caps splashed over the frightened children's heads.

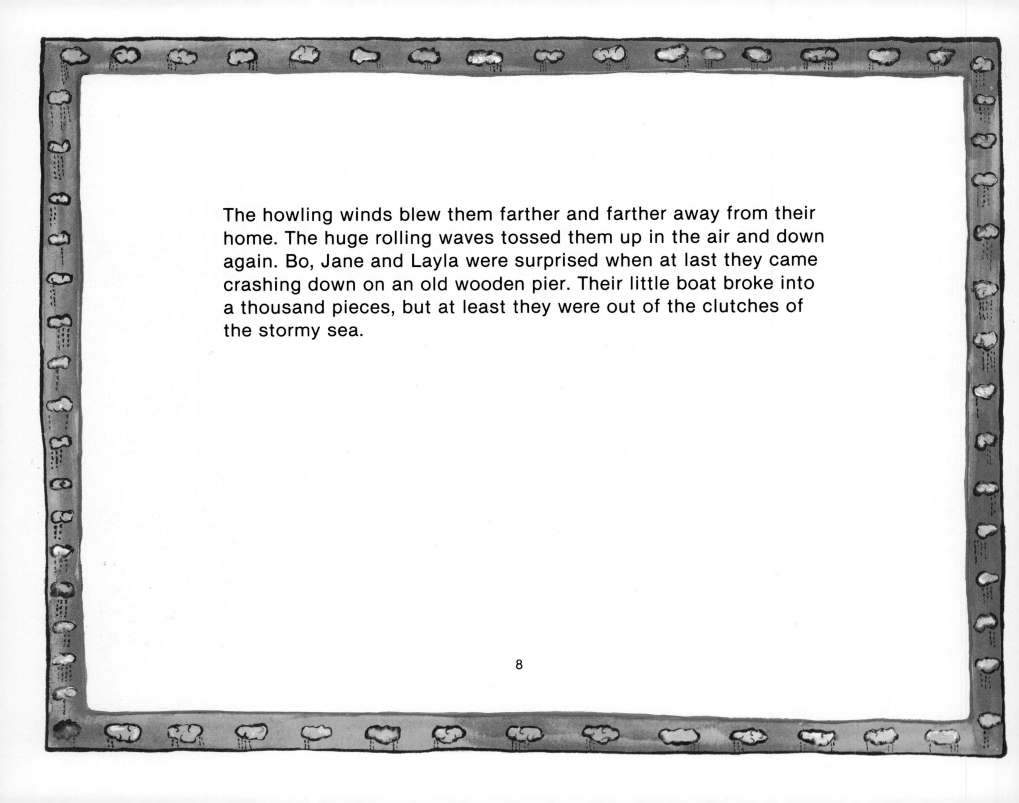

The howling winds blew them farther and farther away from their home. The huge rolling waves tossed them up in the air and down again. Bo, Jane and Layla were surprised when at last they came crashing down on an old wooden pier. Their little boat broke into a thousand pieces, but at least they were out of the clutches of the stormy sea.

'Look, I think we've landed on Redonda!' shouted Bo.

By now it had grown dark, the stars were twinkling in a clear sky and the moon shone down on the little island.

'There's an old house,' Layla said. 'Let's go inside.'

It was empty. It had been abandoned when the King and all the people of Redonda had fled in fear of the old volcano that was always spitting out fire and rocks. The children huddled together and eventually fell asleep, weary from the day's adventure.

In the morning Bo, Jane and Layla peeked out of the window of their shelter and looked out over Redonda and discovered that it was just a little rock in the middle of the big Caribbean Sea.

'Perhaps we can find a boat to take us home,' suggested Jane. 'If we go to the top of that old volcano, then we will be able to see all around us.'

Suddenly, there was a terrific roar and the ground began to shake with a fierce rumbling. 'Ro-o--ar--------o--o-oh!' And out of the volcano burst a ball of fire and rocks. 'Ro-o--ar--------o--o-oh!' A tongue of red and orange fire licked out at the sky again. Rocks flew into the air and landed at the children's feet.

The children ran as fast as they could for the little house and hid behind the door. Peeking up at the angry volcano, they heard a very strange noise indeed.

'Ssshhh,' Layla whispered. 'Listen.'

'O-oh-oh! Sob, sob, sob,' the children heard as they watched the fire and smoke blow away with the wind.

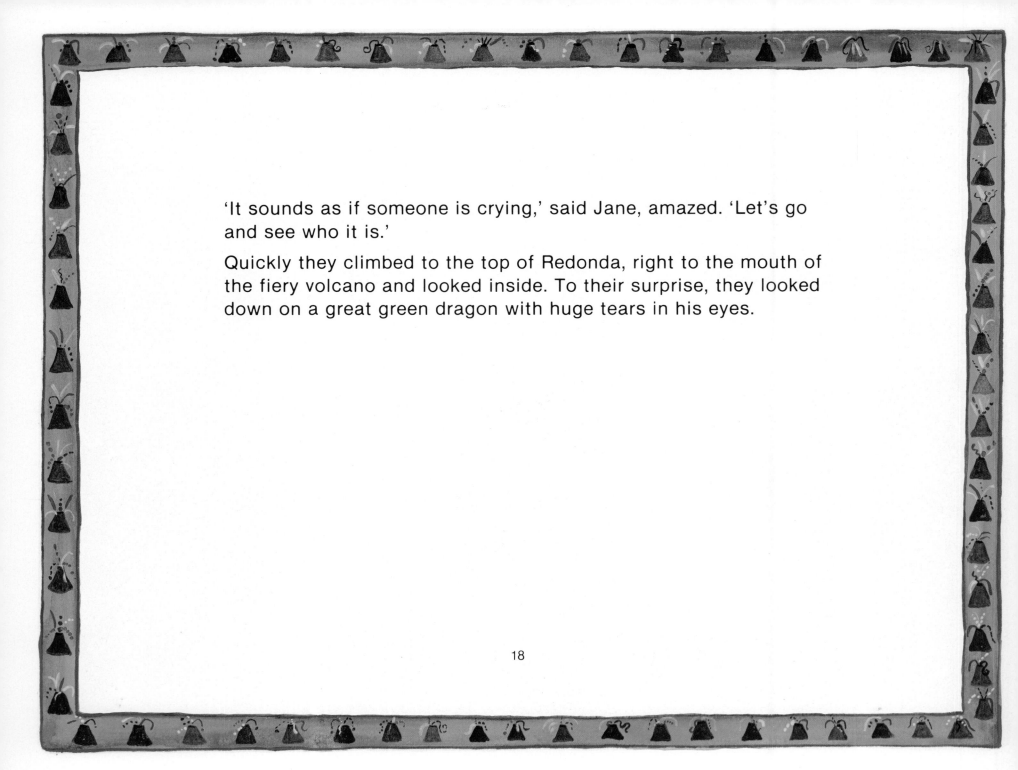

'It sounds as if someone is crying,' said Jane, amazed. 'Let's go and see who it is.'

Quickly they climbed to the top of Redonda, right to the mouth of the fiery volcano and looked inside. To their surprise, they looked down on a great green dragon with huge tears in his eyes.

'Who are you and why are you crying?' Bo asked the dragon.

'My name is Rupert, and I'm stuck in this old volcano. When I was small I swam in here to hide,' wept the dragon. 'Now I'm too big to swim out of the bottom and too small to reach the top.'

'The King of Redonda left with all the people and now lives far, far away. He wants to keep the island for all the animals and birds, but I'm afraid that he's forgotten about me,' Rupert went on, breathing fire with each word. 'And who are you?'

'I'm Bo, and here are Jane and Layla. We were lost in a storm and can't get home again.'

'We'll help you get out!' decided the determined Layla.

'I'll try to hold my fire, if you would only help me,' sobbed Rupert. So the dragon stretched as high as he could so that the children could step on to his head. Then he lowered them gently to the ground.

'Rupert, you really have such lovely big eyes and such a funny red tongue, too. But what are these up here? Are they wings?' asked Jane.

'Yes, all dragons have them although I don't know why,' he said.

'Why don't you use them to fly out of here?' asked Layla brightly.

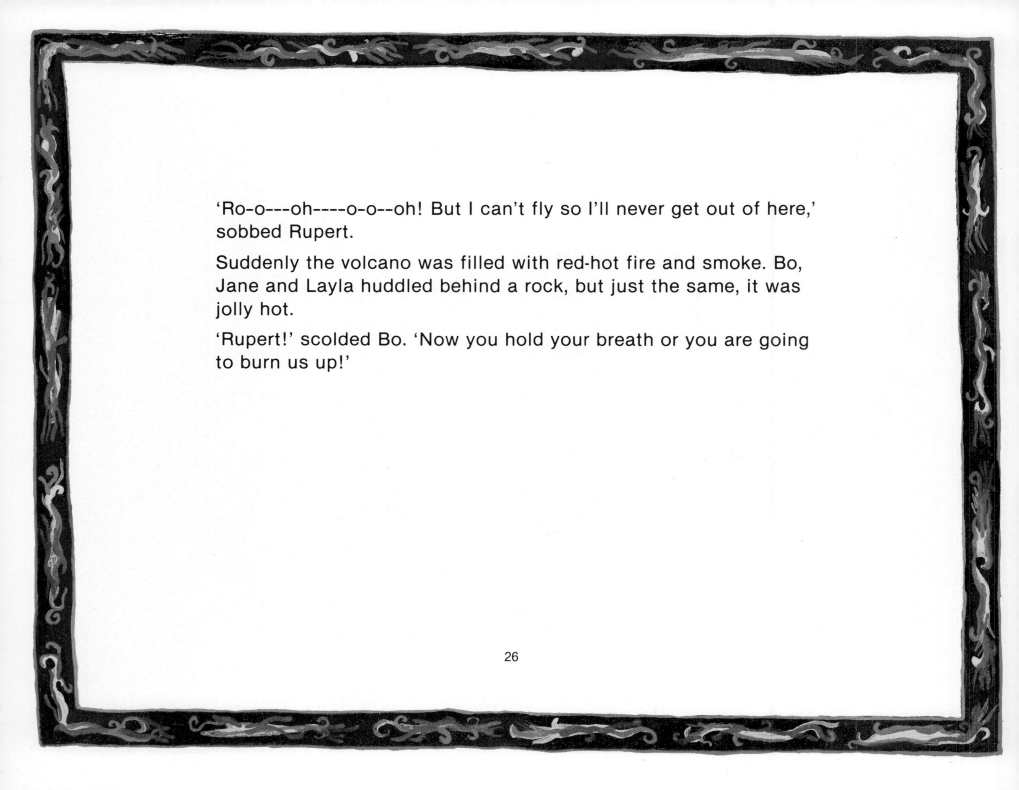

'Ro-o---oh----o-o--oh! But I can't fly so I'll never get out of here,' sobbed Rupert.

Suddenly the volcano was filled with red-hot fire and smoke. Bo, Jane and Layla huddled behind a rock, but just the same, it was jolly hot.

'Rupert!' scolded Bo. 'Now you hold your breath or you are going to burn us up!'

'I'm sorry ... It's just that I don't think I can ever learn to fly,' said the dragon sadly, 'and who would teach me anyway?'

'I will,' said a big white pelican perched at the opening of the volcano. 'My name is Aleph, and I can teach you to fly.'

'Yes, yes!' cried all the excited children, jumping up and down.

Aleph glided down and landed next to Rupert. 'This is what you have to do,' he said.

The pelican stood on his webbed toes and, lifting his great wings gracefully, waved them up and down. Slowly his feet left the ground and the bird floated upwards. From the top of the volcano the bird said, 'Now you try.'

The dragon closed his eyes and flapped his wings up and down, up and down. Nothing happened at all.

'That was very good,' praised Aleph. 'But you are going to have to try harder.'

So once more Rupert lifted up his wings and flapped a little harder. And still he didn't fly.

'Ro-o--ar----------o--o--oh!' he cried.

Giving up, the dragon complained, 'This will never work. Oh dear, I guess I'm stuck in here forever.'

'Don't give up so soon,' said the great white bird. 'It takes time and practice to do anything well – if you keep trying, you will fly.'

Rupert wasn't sure if dragons were supposed to fly. He did know that he wanted to see the rest of the world some day, and find the King of Redonda, and he never would if he was stuck at the bottom of a volcano. So he watched Aleph again carefully as the bird lifted his wings a second time and moved them up and down.

Rupert raised his wings and, standing on his tippy-toes, he flapped as hard as he could. Up and down, up and down, and very slowly the dragon was lifted off the ground. He was so excited that he forgot to keep moving his wings, and with a *THUD*! he came back crashing to the ground.

'Hurrah! Hurrah!' shouted the children and pelican together. 'You can do it! You can really fly!'

'Soon you'll be out into the sunshine,' Layla told the dragon excitedly.

So once again Rupert lifted his wings, and flapped and flapped. Up and down, up and down. His feet left the ground and he went up, up and up. He was nearly at the top of his volcano when he looked down and saw his cheering friends. Rupert was pleased with himself, and he smiled for the first time in many years.

'I'm so happy,' he beamed. 'Now I'll be able to go and see so many wonderful places. If you climb on to my back, I can even take you home.'

So Bo, Jane and Layla hopped on to the dragon's back, and sat between his great green scales. Up and down, up and down. Soon all of them were flying up and up to the top of the volcano and into the bright sunshine.

'Hurrah for Rupert!' sang the children and Aleph. 'Now you are free!'

Indeed Rupert was free, soaring over Redonda where he had lived for so long. In a way he was sad to be leaving his home, but he looked forward to all the places he would soon visit, all the new friends he was going to make, and maybe he could finally meet the King.

'Ro-o-ar! Ro--o--or!' he bellowed, sending sheets of flame over Redonda one last time.

They all took one last look at the island and waved goodbye as they headed home. 'Ro-oar!' Rupert flapped his wings, up and down, going higher and higher until Redonda was just a tiny dot in the big blue sea.